ALSEK'S ABC Adventure

Chris Caldwell

LOST MOOSE

THE YUKON PUBLISHERS

1996

Published by Lost Moose, the Yukon Publishers
58 Kluane Crescent
Whitehorse, Yukon, Canada Y1A 3G7
phone (403) 668-5076, 668-3441, fax (403) 668-6223
e-mail: lmoose@yknet.yk.ca
Web site: http://www.yukonweb.com/business/lost_moose

Canadian Cataloguing in Publication Data
Caldwell, Chris, 1958-
   Alsek's ABC adventure

ISBN 1-896758-00-2
1. Grizzly bear--Yukon Territory--Juvenile fiction.
2. English language--Alphabet--Juvenile literature. I. Title
PS8555.A48A8 1996   jC813'.54   C96-910266-6
PZ7.C12718A1 1996

Design by Mike Rice
Production by K-L Services, Whitehorse

Printed and bound in Canada

The name "Alsek" is taken from the wild Alsek River in southwestern Yukon.

Lost Moose, the Yukon Publishers
To order more copies of this book, or for your free catalogue of books "from the North about the North," contact us at the address above.

The aurora arcs above the arctic alpine as
Alsek awakes with an awesome appetite.

Bb

Bears love berries!

Boundless berry bushes become bountiful
breakfasts for bears' big bellies!

Cc

Alsek considers climbing the cache.
Could it contain cupcakes or cookies?

Dd

The dutiful dog defends the door from disturbance and destruction! Duck!

Alsek energetically exits the encampment.

He eagerly explores an eagle's nest.
Alsek enjoys eating eggs.

Ff

Feathers fly furiously!
Forget it, fuzzball!

Alsek favours a feast of flavourful fish.
Frisky fins fight fiercely for freedom
with a forceful flap in the face!

Gg

A gang of grizzlies gawk and giggle,
getting this griz grumpy!

Grouse are grubbing for gravel.
Alsek grabs greedily.

Hh

Hey! Horses and humans hiking over the hill.
Hurry and hide!

Ii

Isabel and Isaac imagine idyllic days at Inconnu Lake.

Itchy, twitchy and swishy, itty-bitty
insects are incredibly irritating!

Jj

The jumbled jackpines jiggle.
Joker jerks and jumps.

Kk

Koko kicks.
The kitchen kettle
klangs and klunks.

Ll

Lumpy lunges, loosening the leadrope. Leaping
and lurching, he looks to leg it lickety-split.

Mm

Moving madly, Isaac manages a mittful
of mane as Mindy motors by!

Nn

Neatly, Alsek nabs the nearby knapsack. Are nice nibbly nuggets nestled within?

Odd objects roll out. Oh, oh, obstinate dog!

Pp

Pursued by the
persistent pooch,
Alsek plows
through pines,
pelting past
petrified ponies...

...and quickly squirms up a quivering tree.

Rr
Running rapidly to the rescue,
Isabel readies her rifle!

Ss

Suddenly she smiles and shoulders her shooter:

"Let's scram, Sam. This sassy scoundrel is scared silly!"

Tt

The two twins untangle the terrified trotters and take to the trail.

Uu

Upset squirrels utter unprintable insults upon Alsek!

V v

The vanquished
vandal views
the vanguard
vanishing up
the valley.

A wandering wolf, watching
warily, wonders what wacky
weirdness went on here!

W w

Xx Alsek's exhausted from his exciting experiences.

Yawning, he yields to the yellow Yukon sun. **Yy**

Zz

Snoozing in the hazy heat, Alsek
zealously dreams of zesty feasts!

Hey kids! Hey parents!
See how many words you can find on each letter page.

A
airplane
antlers
aurora

B
balloon
baseball
basket
bears
beavers
berries
bibs
birds
bluebirds
bluejays
bow
bowling balls
branches
bread
bunnies
burrow
bushes
butter

C
cabin
cache
canine
canoe
cans
car
caribou
cat
chain
chair
chicken
chimney
corral

D
dandelions
dog
duck

E
eagle
eaglets
ears
elk
evergreen
eyes

F
faces
fall
feathers
feet
fins
fish
fishing rod
fly
fox
fur

G
glaciers
grass
grasshopper
gravel
grizzlies
grouse

H
hare
harness
hat
hawk
hills
hoof
horses
humans

I
insects

J
jam
jar
Joker
jug

K
kettle
kite
knapsack
Koko

L
ladle
lantern
lariat
leather
leaves
legs
lemons
letter
lettuce
lime
Lumpy
lynx

M
magpie
mane
Mindy
moose
mosquitoes
moss
mushrooms

N
nails
name
nest
nose

O
ocarina
oil can
olives
opener
oranges
overcoat
owl

P
pack
pile
porcupine

Q
quills
quilt

R
rabbit
raven
rifle
rocking chair
rocks

S
Sam
sapling
shirt
shoulder
snout
spruce
squirrel
sun

T
table
tarps
towel
trees
tub
twins

U
umbrella
underbrush

V
valley
vanity
vase
view

W
water
wolf

Y
yawn

Z
*features the
entire alphabet*
antler
berries
cupcakes
dandelions
eggs
fish
gravy
hair
ice cream
jar
kettle
ladle
milk
napkin
oranges
pancakes
quilt
rabbit
syrup
turkey
umbrella
violin
waffles
xylophone
yak
zebra